Mrs. Brooks

Zophiel

Mrs. Brooks

Zophiel

1st Edition | ISBN: 978-3-75236-586-3

Place of Publication: Frankfurt am Main, Germany

Year of Publication: 2020

Outlook Verlag GmbH, Germany.

ZOPHIEL,

A Poem,
By Mrs. Brooks.

PREFACE.

Wishing to make a continued effort, in an art which, though almost in secret, has been adored and assiduously cultivated from earliest infancy, it was my intention to have chosen some incident from Pagan history, as the foundation of my contemplated poem. But, looking over the Jewish annals, I was induced to select for my purpose, one of their well-known stories which besides its extreme beauty, seemed to open an extensive field for the imagination which might therein avail itself not only of important and elevated truths but pleasing and popular superstitions.

Having finished one Canto I left the United States for the West Indies in the hope of being able to sail thence for Great Britain, where I might submit what I had done to the candour of some able writer; publish it, if thought expedient; and obtain advice and materials for the improvement and prosecution of my work. But as events have transpired to frustrate that intention I have endeavored to make it as perfect, as with the means I have access to, is possible.

It is, now, far beneath what might have been done, under the influence of more decided hopes and more auspicious circumstances. Yet, as it is, I am induced to place it before the public, with that anxiety which naturally attends the doubtful accomplishment of any favourite object, on the principle that no artist can make the same improvement, or labour with so much pleasure to himself, in private, as when comparing his efforts with those of others, and listening to the opinions of critics and the remarks of connoisseurs. The beauty, though she may view herself, in her mirror, from the ringlets of her hair to the sole of her slipper, and appear most lovely to her own gaze, can never be certain of her power to please until the suffrage of society confirm the opinion formed in seclusion; and "Qu'est ce que la beaute s'elle ne touche pas?"

Literary employments are necessary to the happiness and almost to the vitality of those who pursue them with much ardour; and though the votaries of the muses are, too often, debased by faults, yet, abstractedly considered, a taste for any art, if well directed, must seem a preservative not only against melancholy, but even against misery and vice.

Genius, whatever its bent, supposes a refined and delicate moral sense and though sometimes perverted by sophistry or circumstance, and sometimes failing through weakness; can always, at least, comprehend and feel, the grandeur of honour and the beauty of virtue.

As to the faults of those to whom the world allows the possession of genius, there are, perhaps, good grounds for the belief that they have actually fewer than those employed about ordinary affairs; but the last are easily concealed and the first carefully dragged to light.

The miseries too, sometimes attendant to persons of distinguished literary attainments, are often held forth as a subject of "warn and scare" but Cervantes and Camoens would both have been cast into prison even though unable to read or write, and Savage, though a mechanic or scrivener, would probably have possessed the same failings and consequently have fallen into the same, or a greater degree of poverty and suffering. Alas! how many, in the flower of youth and strength, perish in the loathsome dungeons of this island, and, when dead, are refused a decent grave; who, in many instances, were their histories traced by an able pen would be wept by half the civilized world.

Although I can boast nothing but an extreme and unquenchable love for the art to which my humble aspirations are confined, my lyre has been a solace when every thing else has failed; soothing when agitated, and when at peace furnishing that exercise and excitement without which the mind becomes sick, and all her faculties retrograde when they ought to be advancing. Men, when they feel that nature has kindled in their bosoms a flame which must incessantly be fed, can cultivate eloquence and exert it, in aid of the unfortunate before the judgment seats of their country; or endeavour to "lure to the skies" such as enter the temples of their god; but woman, alike subject to trials and vicissitudes and endowed with the same wishes, (for the observation, "there is no sex to soul," is certainly not untrue,) condemned, perhaps, to a succession of arduous though minute duties in which, oftentimes, there is nothing to charm and little to distract, unless she be allowed the exercise of her pen must fall into melancholy and despair, and perish, (to use the language of Mad. de Stael,) "consumed by her own energies."

Thus do we endeavour to excuse any inordinate or extreme attachment by labouring to show in their highest colours the merits of its object.

Zophiel may or may not be called entirely a creature of imagination, as comports with the faith of the reader; he is not, however, endowed with a single miraculous attribute; for which the general belief of ages, even among christians, may not be produced as authority.

The stanza in which his story is told though less complicate and beautiful than the Spencerian, is equally ancient; and favorable to a pensive melody, is also susceptible of much variety.

The marginal notes will be useless to such as have read much.

San Patricio, Island of Cuba, March 30, 1825.

INVOCATION.

Thou with the dark blue eye upturned to heaven,
And cheek now pale, now warm with radiant glow,
    Daughter of God,—most dear,—
    Come with thy quivering tear,
And tresses wild, and robes of loosened flow,—
To thy lone votaress let one look be given!

Come Poesy! nor like some just-formed maid,
With heart as yet unswoln by bliss or woe;—
    But of such age be seen
    As Egypt's glowing queen,
When her brave Roman learned to love her so
That death and loss of fame, were, by a smile, repaid.

Or as thy Sappho, when too fierce assailed
By stern ingratitude her tender breast:—
    Her love by scorn repaid
    Her friendship true betrayed,
Sick of the guileful earth, she sank for rest
In the cold waves embrace; while Grecian muse bewailed.

Be to my mortal eye, like some fair dame—
Ripe, but untouched by time; whose frequent blush
    Plays o'er her cheek of truth
    As soft as earliest youth;
While thoughts exalted to her mild eye rush—
And the expanded soul, tells 'twas from heaven it came.

Daughter of life's first cause; who, when he saw
The ills that unborn innocents must bear,
    When doomed to come to earth—
    Bethought—and gave thee birth
To charm the poison from affliction there;
And from his source eternal, bade thee draw.

He gave thee power, inferior to his own
But in control o'er matter. 'Mid the crash
    Of earthquake, war, and storm,
    Is seen thy radiant form
Thou com'st at midnight on the lightning's flash,
And ope'st to those thou lov'st new scenes and worlds unknown.

And still, as wild barbarians fiercely break
The graceful column and the marble dome—
     Where arts too long have lain
     Debased at pleasure's fain,
And bleeding justice called on wrath to come,
'Mid ruins heaped around, thou bidst thy votarists wake.

Methinks I see thee on the broken shrine
Of some fall'n temple—where the grass waves high
     With many a flowret wild;
     While some lone, pensive, child
Looks on the sculpture with a wondering eye
Whose kindling fires betray that he is chosen thine. [FN#1]

[FN#1] Genius, perhaps, has often, nay generally, been awakened and the
whole future bent of the mind thus strongly operated upon, determined, by
some circumstance trivial as this.

Or on some beetling cliff—where the mad waves
Rush echoing thro' the high-arched caves below,
     I view some love-reft fair
     Whose sighing warms the air,
Gaze anxious on the ocean as it raves
And call on thee-alone, of power to sooth her woe.

Friend of the wretched; smoother of the couch
Of pining hope; thy pitying form I know!
     Where thro' the wakeful night,
     By a dim taper's light,
Lies a pale youth, upon his pallet low,
Whose wan and woe-worn charms rekindle at thy touch.

Friendless—oppressed by fate—the restless fires
Of his thralled soul prey on his beauteous frame—
     Till, strengthened by thine aid,
     He shapes some kindred maid,
Pours forth in song the life consuming flame,
And for awhile forgets his sufferings and desires.

Scorner of thoughtless grandeur, thou hast chose
Thy *best-beloved* from ruddy Nature's breast:
     The grotto dark and rude—
     The forest solitude—
The craggy mount by blushing clouds carest—
Have altars where thy light etherial glows. [FN#2]

[FN#2] Every nation, however rude, has, as it has been justly observed, a taste for poetry. This art after all that has and can be said for and against it, is the language of nature, and among the relics of the most polished and learned nations little has survived except such as simply depicts those natural feelings and images which have ever existed and ever must continue. Most of the great poets have been individuals of humble condition rising from the mass of the people by that natural principle which causes the most etherial particles to rise and the denser to sink to the earth. But, as Byron exquisitely says, in one of the most wonderfully beautiful pages he ever composed,

"Many are poets who have never penned
Their inspirations, and, perchance, the best;
They felt, they loved, and died; but would not lend
Their thoughts to meaner beings; they comprest
The god within them, and rejoined the stars
Unlaurel'd upon earth."

In the place where I now write amid several hundred Africans of different ages, and nations, the most debased of any on the face of the earth, I have been enabled to observe, even in this, last link of the chain of humanity, the strong natural love for music and poetry.

Any little incident which occurs on the estate where they toil, and which the greater part of them are never suffered to leave, is immediately made the subject of a rude song which they, in their broken Spanish, sing to their companions; and thereby relieve a little the monotony of their lives.

I have observed these poor creatures, under various circumstances, and though, generally, extremely brutal, have, in some instances, heard touches of sentiment from them, when under the influence of grief, equal to any which have flowed from the pen of Rousseau.

Thy sovereign priest by earth's vile sons was driven
To make the cold unconscious earth his bed:[FN#3]
    The damp cave mocked his sighs—
    But from his sightless eyes,
Wrung forth by wrongs, the anguished drops he shed,
Fell each as an appeal to summon thee from heaven.

Thou sought'st him in his desolation; placed
On thy warm bosom his unpillowed head;
    Bade him for visions live
    More bright than worlds can give;
O'er his pale lips thy soul infusive shed
That left his dust adored where kings decay untraced.

[FN#3] "On the banks of the Meles was shown the spot where Critheis, the mother of Homer, brought him into the world, and the cavern to which he retired to compose his immortal verses. A monument erected to his memory and inscribed with his name stood in the middle of the city—it was adorned with spacious porticos under which the citizens assembled."

Source of deep feeling—of surpassing love—
Creative power,—'tis thou hast peopled heaven
    Since man from dust arose
    His birth the cherub owes [FN#4]
To thee—by thee his rapturous harp was given
And white wings tipp'd with gold that cool the domes above.

[FN#4] The Indians (says M. de Voltaire) from whom every species of theology is derived, invented the angels and represented them in their ancient book the "Shasta," as immortal creatures, participating in the divinity of their creator; against whom a great number revolted in heaven, "Les Parsis ignicoles, qui subsistent encore ont communique a l'auteur de la religion des anciens Perses les noms des anges que les premiers Perses reconnaissaient. On en trouve cent-dix- neuf, parmi desquels ne sont ni Raphael ni Gabriel que les Perses n'adopterent que long-tems apres. Ces mots sont Chaldeens; ils ne furent connus des Juifs que dans leur captivite."

Husher of secret sighs—from childhood's hour
The slave of Fate, I've knelt before thy throne;
    To thy loved courts have sped
    Whene'er my heart has bled,
And every ray of bliss that heart has known
Has reached it thro' thy grief-dispelling power.

Fain thro' my native solitudes I'd roam
Bathe my rude harp in my bright native streams
    Twine it with flowers that bloom
    But for the deserts gloom,
Or, for the long and jetty hair that gleams
O'er the dark-bosomed maid that makes the wild her home. [FN#5]

[FN#5] This invocation when composed was intended to precede a series of poems entitled Occidental Eclogues; which work the writer has never found opportunity to finish.

I sing not for the crowd, or low or high—
A pensive wanderer on life's thorny heath
    Earth's pageants for my view
    Have nought: I love but few,

And few who chance to hear thy trembling breath,
My lyre, for her who wakes thee, have a sigh. [FN#6]

[FN#6] It may not be improper to observe that these stanzas were composed
during a period of misfortune and dejection.

Forsake me not! none ever loved thee more!
Fair queen, I'll meet woe's fearfulest frown—and smile;
    If mid the scene severe
    Thou'lt drop on me one tear,
And let thy flitting form sometimes beguile
The present of its ills—I'll scorn them and adore.

Then warm the form relentless fate would chill—
Dark lours my night—Oh! give me one embrace!
    If every pain I bear
    Befit me for thy care,
Come sorrow—scorn—desertion—I can chase
Despair, fell watching for her victim still.

ZOPHIEL.

CANTO I.

I.

The time has been—this holiest records say—
In punishment for crimes of mortal birth,
When spirits banished from the realms of day
Wandered malignant o'er the nighted earth.(1)

And from the cold and marble lips declared,
Of some blind-worshipped—earth-created god,
Their deep deceits; which trusting monarchs snared
Filling the air with moans, with gore the sod. [FN#7]

Yet angels doffed their robes in radiance dyed,
And for a while the joys of heaven delayed,
To watch benign by some just mortal's side—
Or meet th' aspiring love of some high gifted maid. [FN#8]

Blest were those days!—can these dull ages boast
Aught to compare? tho' now no more beguile—
Chain'd in their darkling depths th' infernal host—
Who would not brave a fiend to share an angel's smile?

[FN#7] The god who conducted the Hebrews sent a malignant spirit to speak
from the mouth of the prophets, in order to deceive king Achab.

[FN#8] It is useless to note this stanza, as two well-known poems have lately
been founded on the same passage of the Pentateuch to which it alludes.

II.

'Twas then there lived a captive Hebrew pair;
In woe th' embraces of their youth had past,
And blest their paler years one daughter—fair
She flourished, like a lonely rose, the last

And loveliest of her line. The tear of joy—
The early love of song—the sigh that broke
From her young lip—the best-beloved employ—
What womanhood disclosed in infancy bespoke.

A child of passion—tenderest and best
Of all that heart has inly loved and felt;
Adorned the fair enclosure of her breast—
Where passion is not found, no virtue ever dwelt.

Yet not, perverted, would my words imply
The impulse given by Heaven's great Artizan
Alike to man and worm—mere spring, whereby
The distant wheels of life, while time endures, roll on—

But the collective ministry that fill
About the soul, their all-important place—

That feed her fires—empower her fainting will—
And write the god on feeble mortals face.

III.

Yet anger, or revenge, envy or hate
The damsel knew not: when her bosom burned
And injury darkened the decrees of fate,
She had more pitious wept to see that pain returned.

Or if, perchance, tho' formed most just and pure,
Amid their virtue's wild luxuriance hid,
Such germ all mortal bosoms must immure
Which sometimes show their poisonous heads unbid—

If haply such the lovely Hebrew finds,
Self knowledge wept th' abasing truth to know,
And *innate pride,* that *queen of noble minds,*
Crushed them indignant ere a bud could grow.

IV.

And such—ev'n now, in earliest youth are seen—
But would they live, with armour more deform,
Their love—o'erflowing breasts must learn to screen:
"The bird that sweetest sings can least endure the storm."

V.

And yet, despite of all the gushing tear—
The melting tone—the darting heart-stream—proved,
The soul that in them spoke, could spurn at fear
Of death or danger; and had those she loved

Required it at their need, she could have stood,
Unmoved, as some fair-sculptured statue, while
The dome that guards it, earth's convulsions, rude
Are shivering—meeting ruin with a smile.

VI.

And this, at intervals in language bright
Told her blue eyes; tho' oft the tender lid
Like lilly drooping languidly; and white
And trembling—all save love and lustre hid.

Then, as young christian bard had sung, they seemed
Like some Madonna in his soul—so sainted;
But opening in their energy—they beamed
As tasteful pagans their Minerva painted;

While o'er her graceful shoulders' milky swell,
Like those full oft on little children seen
Almost to earth her silken ringlets fell
Nor owned Pactolus' sands more golden sheen.

VII.

And now, full near, the hour unwished for drew
When fond, Sephora hoped to see her wed;
And, for 'twould else expire, impatient grew
To renovate her race from beauteous Egla's bed.

VIII.

None of their kindred lived to claim her hand
But stranger-youths had asked her of her sire
With gifts and promise fair; he could withstand
All save her tears; and harkening her desire

Still left her free; but soon her mother drew
From her a vow, that when the twentieth year
Its full, fair finish o'er her beauty threw,
If what her fancy fed on, came not near,

She would entreat no more but to the voice
Of her light-giver hearken; and her life
And love—all yielding to that kindly choice
Would hush each idle wish and learn to be a wife.

IX.

Now oft it happ'd when morning task was done
And for the virgins of her household made
And lotted each her toil; while yet the sun
Was young, fair Egla to a woody shade,

Loved to retreat; there, in the fainting hour
Of sultry noon the burning sunbeam fell
Like a warm twilight; so bereft of power,
It gained an entrance thro' the leafy bower;
That scarcely shrank the tender lilly bell

Tranquil and lone in such a light to be,
How sweet to sense and soul!—the form recline
Forgets it ere felt pain; and reverie,
Sweet mother of the muses, heart and soul are thine. [FN#9]

[FN#9] Every one talks and reads of groves, but it is impossible for those who never felt it, to conceive the effect of such a situation in a warm climate. In this island the woods which are naturally so interwoven with vines as to be impervious to a human being, are in some places, cleared and converted into nurseries for the young coffee-trees which remain sheltered from the sun and wind till sufficiently grown to transplant. To enter one of these "semilleros," as they are here called, at noon day, produces an effect like that anciently ascribed to the waters of Lethe. After sitting down upon the trunk of a fallen cedar or palm-tree, and breathing for a moment, the freshness of the air and the odour of the passion flower, which is one of the most abundant, and certainly the most beautiful of the climate; the noise of the trees, which are continually kept in motion by the trade winds; the fluttering and various notes, though not musical, of the birds; the loftiness of the green canopy, for the trunks of the trees are bare to a great height, and seem like pillars supporting the thick mass of leaves above; and the rich mellow light which the intense rays of the sun, thus impeded, produce; have altogether such an effect that one involuntarily forgets every thing but the present, and it requires a strong effort to rise and leave the place.

X.

This calm recess on summer day she sought
And sat to tune her lute; but all night long
Quiet had from her pillow flown, and thought
Feverish and tired, sent for th' unseemly throng

Of boding images. She scarce could woo
One song reluctant, ere advancing quick
Thro' the fresh leaves Sephora's form she knew
And duteous rose to meet; but fainting sick

Her heart sank tremulously in her; why
Sought out at such an hour, it half divined
And seated now beside, with downcast eye
And fevered pulse, she met the pressure, kind

And warmly given; while thus the matron fair
Nor yet much marr'd by time, with soothing words
Solicitous; and gently serious air
The purpose why she hither came preferr'd:

XI.

"Egla, my hopes thou knowest—tho' exprest
But rare lest they should pain thee—I have dealt
Not rudely towards thee tender; and supprest
The wish, of all, my heart has most vehement felt.

"Know I have marked, that when the reason why
Thou still wouldst live in virgin state, thy sire
Has prest thee to impart, quick in thine eye
Semblance of hope has played—fain to transpire

"Words seem'd to seek thy lip; but the bright rush
Of heart-blood eloquent, alone would tell
In the warm language of a rebel blush
What thy less treacherous tongue has guarded well.

XII.

"Dost waste so oft alone—the cheerful day?
Or haply, rather bath some pagan youth"—
She with quick burst—'whate'er has happ'd I'll say!
Doubt thou my wisdom, but regard my truth!

XIII.

"Long time ago, while yet a twelve years' child
These shrubs and vines, new planted, near this spot,
I sat me tired with pleasant toil, and whiled
Away the time with many a wishful thought

"Of desolate Judea. Every scene
Which thou so oft, while sitting on thy knee,
Wouldst sing of, weeping, thro' my mind has been
Successive; when from yon old mossy tree

"I heard a pitious moan. Wondering I went
And found a wretched man; worn and opprest
He seemed with toil and years; and whispering faint
He said "Oh little maiden, sore distrest

"I sink for very want. Give me I pray,
A drop of water and a cake: I die
Of thirst and hunger, yet my sorrowing way
May tread once more, if thou my needs supply."

XIV.

"A long time missing from thy fondling arms—
It chanced that day thou'dst sent me in the shade
New bread, a cake of figs, and wine of palms [FN#10]
Mingled with water, sweet with honey made.

"These did I bring—raised as I could, his head;
Held to his lip the cup; and while he quaffed,
Upon my garment wiped the tears that sped
Adown his silvery beard and mingled with the draft.

[FN#10] "The palm is a very common plant in this country, (Assyria,) and generally fruitful; this they cultivate like fig-trees and it produces them bread, wine and honey." See Beloe's notes to his translation of Herodotus. Mr. Gibbon adds, that the diligent natives celebrated, either in verse or prose, three hundred and sixty uses to which the trunk, the branches, the leaves, the juice and the fruit of this plant were applied. Nothing can be more curious and interesting than the natural history of the palm tree.

XV.

"When gaining sudden strength, he raised his hand,

And in this guise did bless me, "Mayst thou be
A crown to him who weds thee.—In a land
Far distant bides a captive. Hearken me

"And choose thee now a bridegroom meet: to day
O'er broad Euphrates' steepest banks a child
Fled from his youthful nurse's arms; in play
Elate, he bent him o'er the brink, and smiled

"To see their fears who followed him—but who
The keen wild anguish of that scene can tell—
He bend o'er the brink, and in their view,
But ah! too far beyond their aid—he fell.

XVI.

"They wailed—the long torn ringlets of their hair [FN#11]
Freighted the pitying gale; deep rolled the stream
And swallowed the fair child; no succour there—
They women—whither look—who to redeem

"What the fierce waves were preying on?—when lo!
Approached a stranger boy. Aside he flung,
As darted thought, his quiver and his bow
And parted by his limbs the sparkling billows sung.

[FN#11] The women, I believe, among all nations of antiquity were
accustomed to express violent grief by tearing their hair. This must have been
a great and affecting sacrifice to the object bemoaned, as they considered it a
part of themselves and absolutely essential to their beauty. Fine hair has been
a subject of commendation among all people, and particularly the ancients.
Cyrus, when he went to visit his uncle Astyages found him with his eyelashes
coloured, and decorated with false locks; the first Caesar obtained permission
to wear the laurel-wreath in order to conceal the bareness of his temples. The
quantity and beauty of the hair of Absalom is commemorated in holy writ.
The modern oriental ladies also set the greatest value on their hair which they
braid and perfume. Thus says the poet Hafiz, whome Sir William Jones styles
the Anacreon of Persia,

"Those locks, each curl of which is worth a hundred musk-bags of China,
would be sweet indeed, if their scent proceeded from sweetness of temper."

and again,

"When the breeze shall waft the fragrance of thy locks over the tomb of

Hafiz, a thousand flowers shall spring from the earth that hides his corse."

Achilles clipped his yellow locks and threw them as a sacrifice upon the funeral pyre of Patroclus.

XVII.

"They clung to an old palm and watched; nor breath
Nor word dared utter; while the refluent flood
Left on each countenance the hue of death,
Ope'd lip and far strained eye spoke worse than death endured.

XVIII.

"But, down the flood, the dauntless boy appeared,—
Now rising—plunging—in the eddy whirled—
Mastering his course—but now a rock he neared—
And closing o'er his head, the deep, dark waters curled.

"Then Hope groaned forth her last; and drear despair
Spoke in a shriek; but ere its echo wild
Had ceased to thrill; restored to light and air—
He climbs, he gains the rock, and holds alive the child.

XIX.

"Now mark what chanced—that infant was the son
E'vn of the king of Nineveh: and placed
Before him was the youth who so had won
From death the royal heir. A captive graced

"All o'er with Nature's gifts he sparkled—brave
And panting for renown—blushing and praised
The stripling stood; and closely prest, would crave
Alone a place mid warlike men; and raised

"To his full wish, the kingly presence left,
Buoyant and bright with hope; dreaming of nought
While revelled his full soul in visions deft,
But blessings from his sire and pleasures of a court.

17

XX.

"But when his mother heard, she wept; and said
If he our only child be far away
Or slain in war; how shall our years be stayed?
Friendless and old, where is the hand to lay

"Our white hairs in the earth?—So when her fears
He saw would not be calmed, he did not part,
But lived in low estate, to dry her tears,
And crushed the full-grown-hopes, exulting at his heart."

XXI.

"The old man ceased; ere I could speak, his face
Grew more than mortail fair: a mellow light
Mantling around him fill'd the shady place
And while I wondering stood; he vanished from my sight.

XXII.

"This I had told,—but shame withheld—and fear
Thou'dst deem some spirit guilded me—disapprove—
Perchance forbid my customed wanderings here;
But whencesoe'er the vision, I have strove

"Still vainly to forget—I've heard the mourn
Kindred afar, and captive—oh! my mother—
Should he—my heaven announced—exist, return—
And meet me drear—lost—wedded to another"—

Then thus Sephora, "In the city where
Our kindred distant dwelt—blood has been shed—
Dreamer, had such heroic boy been there,
Belike he's numbered with the silent dead.

"Or doth he live he knows not—would not know
(Thralled—dead, to thee—in fair Assyrian arms.)
Who pines for him afar in fruitless woe
A phantom's bride—wasting love, life and charms.

XXIII.

"'Tis as a vine of Galilee should say,
Culturer, I reck not thy support, I sigh
For a young palm tree, of Euphrates; nay—
Or let me him entwine or in my blossom die.

"Thy heart is set on joys it may not prove,
And, panting ingrate, scorns the blessings given?—
Hoping from dust formed man, a seraph's love
And days on earth like to the days of heaven.

XXIV.

"But to my theme, maiden, a lord for thee,
And not of thee unworthy—I have chose—
Dispel the dread, that in thy looks I see—
Nor make it task of anguish to disclose,

"What should be—thine heart's dew. Remember'st thou
When to the Altar, by thy father reared,
We suppliant went with sacrifice and vow,
A victim-dove escaped? and there appeared

"And would have brought thee others to supply
Its loss, a Median?—thou, dissolved, to praise,
Didst note the beauty of his shape and eye,
And, as he parted, in the sunny rays

"The ringlets of his black locks clustering bright
Around his pillar-neck," "tis pity he'
Thou saidst, 'in all the comeliness and might
Of perfect man—pity like him, should be

"But an idolater: how nobly sweet
He tempereth pride with courtesy; a flower
Drops honey when he speaks. Yet 'twere most meet
To praise his majesty: he stands—a tower.'

"The same, a false idolater no more,
Now bows him to the God, for whose dread ire
Fall'n on us loved but sinning, we deplore
This long but just captivity. Thy sire

"Receives him well and harkens his request

For know, he comes to ask thee-for a bride
And to be one among a people, blest
Tho' deep in suffering. Nor to him denied

"Art thou, sad daughter—weep—if't be thy will—
E'vn on the breast that nourished thee and ne'er
Distrest thee or compelled; this bosom still
Ev'n should'st though blight its dearest hopes, will share

"Nay, bear thy pains; but sooner in the grave
'Twill quench my waning years, if reckless thou
Of what I not command, but only crave,
Let my heart pine regardless of thy vow."

XXV.

She thus, 'O think not, kindest, I forget,
Receiving so much love, how much is due
From me to thee: the Mede I'll wed—but yet
I cannot stay these tears that gush to pain thy view.'

XXVI.

Sephora held her to heart, the while
Grief had its way—then saw her gently laid
And bade her, kissing her blue eyes, beguile
Slumbering the fervid noon. Her leafy bed

Sighed forth o'erpowering breath; increased the heat;
Sleepless had been the night; her weary sense
Could now no more. Lone in the still retreat,
Wounding the flowers to sweetness more intense,

She sank. 'Tis thus, kind Nature lets our woe
Swell 'til it bursts forth from the o'erfraught breast;
Then draws an opiate from the bitter flow,
And lays her sorrowing child soft in the lap to rest.

XXVII.

Now all the mortal maid lies indolent

Save one sweet cheek which the cool velvet turf
Had touched too rude, tho' all the blooms besprent,
One soft arm pillowed. Whiter than the surf

That foams against the sea-rock, looked her neck,
By the dark, glossy, odorous shrubs relieved,
That close inclining o'er her seemed to reck
What 'twas they canopied; and quickly heaved

Beneath her robe's white folds and azure zone,
Her heart yet incomposed; a fillet thro'
Peeped brightly azure, while with tender moan
As if of bliss, Zephyr her ringlets blew

Sportive;—about her neck their gold he twined,
Kissed the soft violet on her temples warm,
And eye brow—just so dark might well define
Its flexile arch;—throne of expression's charm.

XXVIII.

As the vexed Caspian, tho' its rage be past
And the blue smiling heavens swell o'er in peace,
Shook to the centre, by the recent blast,
Heaves on tumultuous still, and hath not power to cease.

So still each little pulse was seen to throb
Tho' passion and its pains were lulled to rest,
And "even and anon" a pitious sob
Shook the pure arch expansive o'er her breast. [FN#12]

[FN#12] This effect is very observable in little children, who for several hours
after they have cried themselves to sleep, and sometimes even when a smile is
on their lips, are heard, from time to time, to utter sobs.

XXIX.

Save that 'twas all tranquillity; that reigned
O'er fragrance sound and beauty; all was mute—
Save when a dove her dear one's absence plained
And the faint breeze mourned o'er the slumberer's lute.

XXX.

It chanced, that day, lured by the verdure, came
Zophiel, now minister of ill; but ere
He sinned, a heavenly angel. The faint flame
Of dying embers, on an altar, where

Raguel, fair Egla's sire, in secret vowed
And sacrificed to the sole living God,
Where friendly shades the sacred rites enshroud;—(2)
The fiend beheld and knew; his soul was awed,

And he bethought him of the forfeit joys
Once his in Heaven;—deep in a darkling grot
He sat him down;—the melancholy noise
Of leaf and creeping vine accordant with his thought.

XXXI.

When fiercer spirits, howled, he but complained (3)
Ere yet 'twas his to roam the pleasant earth,
His heaven-invented harp he still retained
Tho' tuned to bliss no more; and had its birth

Of him, beneath some black infernal clift
The first drear song of woe; and torment wrung
The spirit less severe where he might lift
His plaining voice—and frame the like as now he sung:

XXXII.

"Woe to thee, wild ambition, I employ
Despair's dull notes thy dread effects to tell,
Born in high-heaven, her peace thou could'st destroy,
And, but for thee, there had not been a hell.

"Thro' the celestial domes thy clarion pealed,—
Angels, entranced, beneath thy banners ranged,
And stright were fiends;—hurled from the shrinking field,
They waked in agony to wait the change.

"Darting thro' all her veins the subtle fire
The world's fair mistress first inhaled thy breath,

22

To lot of higher beings learned to aspire,—
Dared to attempt—and doomed the world to death.

"Thy thousand wild desires, that still torment
The fiercely struggling soul, where peace once dwelt,
But perished;—feverish hope—drear discontent,
Impoisoning all possest—Oh! I have felt

"As spirits feel—yet not for man we mourn
Scarce o'er the silly bird in state were he,
That builds his nest, loves, sings the morn's return,
And sleeps at evening; save by aid of thee,

"Fame ne'er had roused, nor song her records kept
The gem, the ore, the marble breathing life,
The pencil's colours,—all in earth had slept,
Now see them mark with death his victim's strife.

"Man found thee death—but death and dull decay
Baffling, by aid of thee, his mastery proves;—
By mighty works he swells his narrow day
And reigns, for ages, on the world he loves.

"Yet what the price? with stings that never cease
Thou goad'st him on; and when, too keen the smart,
He fain would pause awhile—and signs for peace,
Food thou wilt have, or tear his victim heart."

XXXIII.

Thus Zophiel still,—"tho' now the infernal crew
Had gained by sin a privilege in the world,
Allayed their torments in the cool night dew,
And by the dim star-light again their wings unfurled."

XXXIV.

And now, regretful of the joys his birth
Had promised; deserts, mounts and streams he crost,
To find, amid the loveliest spots of earth,
Faint likeness of the heaven he had lost.

And oft, by unsuccessful searching pained,

Weary he fainted thro' the toilsome hours;
And then his mystic nature he sustained
On steam of sacrifices—breath of flowers. (4)

XXXV.

Sometimes he gave out oracles, amused
With mortal folly; resting on the shrines;
Or, all in some fair Sibyl's form infused,
Spoke from her quivering lips, or penned her mystic lines. [FN#13]

[FN#13] This passage merely accords with the belief that the responses of the
ancient oracles were spoken by fiends, or evil spirits. We need only look into
the "New Testament for a confirmation of the power which such beings were
supposed to possess of speaking from the lips of mortals."

XXXVI.

And now he wanders on from glade to glade
To where more precious shrubs diffuse their balms,
And gliding thro' the thick inwoven shade
Where the young Hebrew lay in all her charms,

He caught a glimpse. The colours in her face—
Her bare white arms—her lips—her shining hair—
Burst on his view. He would have flown the place;
Fearing some faithful angel rested there,

Who'd see him—reft of glory—lost to bliss—
Wandering and miserably panting—fain
To glean a scanty joy—with thoughts like this—
Came all he'd known and lost—he writh'd with pain

Ineffable—But what assailed his ear,
A sigh?—surprised, another glance he took;
Then doubting—fearing—gradual coming near—
He ventured to her side and dared to look;

Whispering, "yes, 'tis of earth! So, new-found life
Refreshing, looked sweet Eve, with purpose fell
When first sin's sovereign gazed on her, and strife
Had with his heart, that grieved with arts of hell,

"Stern as it was, to win her o'er to death!—
Most beautiful of all in earth, in heaven,
Oh! could I quaff for aye that fragrant breath
Couldst thou, or being likening thee, be given

"To bloom forever for me thus—still true
To one dear theme, my full soul flowing o'er,
Would find no room for thought of what it knew—
Nor picturing forfeit transport, curse me more. (5)

"But oh! severest pain!—I cannot be
In what I love, blest ev'n the little span—
(With all a spirit's keen capacity
For bliss) permitted the poor insect man.

XXXVII.

"The few I've seen and deemed of worth to win
Like some sweet flowret mildewed, in my arms,
Withered to hidiousness—foul ev'n as sin—
Grew fearful hags; and then with potent charm [FN#14]

[FN#14] One of the most striking absurdities in the lately- dispelled
superstition of witchcraft, is the extreme hidiousness and misery usually
ascribed to such as made use of the agency of evil spirits. I have therefore
made it the result of an unforeseen necessity: no female can be supposed to
purchase, voluntarily, the power of doing mischief to others at the price of
beauty and every thing like happiness on her own part.

"Of muttered word and harmful drug, did learn
To force me to their will. Down the damp grave
Loathing, I went at Endor, and uptorn
Brought back the dead; when tortured Saul did crave,

"To view his pending fate. Fair—nay, as this
Young slumberer, that dread witch; when, I arrayed
In lovely shape, to meet my guileful kiss
She yielded first her lip. And thou, sweet maid—
What is't I see?—a recent tear has strayed
And left its stain upon her cheek of bliss.—

XXXVIII.

"She's fall'n to sleep in grief—haply been chid,
Or by rude mortal wronged. So let it prove
Meet for my purpose: 'mid these blossoms hid,
I'll gaze; and when she wakes with all that love

"And art can lend, come forth. He who would gain
A fond full heart, in love's soft surgery skilled
Should seek it when 'tis sore; allay its pain—
With balm by pity prest 'tis all his own, so healed

XXXIX.

"She may be mine a little year—ev'n fair
And sweet as now—Oh! respite! while possest
I lose the dismal sense of my despair—
But then—I will not think upon the rest.

"And wherefore grieve to cloud her little day [FN#15]
Of fleeting life?—What doom from power divine
I bear eternal! thoughts of ruth, away!
Wake pretty fly!—and—while thou mayst,—be mine.

"Tho' but an hour—so thou suppli'st thy looms
With shining silk, [FN#16] and in the cruel snare
See'st the fond bird entrapped, but for his plumes
To work thy robes, or twine amidst thy hair."

[FN#15] The ancient Hebrews had no idea of a future state.

[FN#16] I have not been able to discover whether the use of silk was known at so early a period. It is said to have been sold in Rome for its weight in gold, and was considered so luxurious an article that it was considered infamous for a man to appear drest in it. The Roman Pausanias says that it came from the country of the Seres, a people of Asiatic Scythia.

XL.

To wisper softly in her ear he bent,
But draws him back restrained: A higher power
That loved to watch o'er slumbering innocent,
Repelled his evil touch; and, from her bower

To lead the maid, Sephora comes; the sprite

Half baffled, followed—hovering on unseen—
Till Meles, fair to see and nobly dight,
Received his pensive bride. Gentle of mien

She meekly stood. He fastened round her arm
Rings of refulgent ore; low and apart
Murmuring, "so beauteous captive, shall thy charms
Forever thrall and clasp thy captive's heart."

The air breathed softer, as she slowly moved
In languid resignation: his quick eye
Spoke in black glances how she was approved,
Who shrunk reluctant from its ardency.

XLI.

'Twas sweet to look upon the goodly pair
In their contrasted loveliness: her height
Might almost vie with his; but heavenly fair,
Of soft proportion she, and sunny hair
He cast in manliest mould with ringlets murk as night.

XLII.

All art could give with Nature's charms was blent,
His gorgeous country shone in his attire,
And as he moved with tread magnificent
She could but look and looking must admire.

XLIII.

And oft her drooping and resigned blue eye
She'd wistful raise to read his radiant face,
But then—why shrank her heart? a secret sigh
Told her it most required what there it could not trace.

XLIV.

Now fair had fall'n the night. The damsel mused

At her own window, in the pearly ray
Of the full moon; her thoughtful soul infused
Thus in her words; left 'lone awhile, to pray.

XLV.

"What bliss for her who lives her little day,
In blest obedience; like to those divine
Who to her loved, her earthly lord, can say
'God is thy law,' most just 'and *thou* art mine.'

"To every blast she bends in beauty meek—
How can she shrink—his arms her shelter kind?—
And feels no need to blanch her rosy cheek
With thoughts befitting his superior mind.

"Who only sorrows when she sees him pained,
Then knows to pluck away pain's fiercest dart;
Or, love arresting, ere its gaol is gained
Steal half its venom ere it reach his heart.

"'Tis the soul's food—the fervid must adore—
For this the heathen, insufficed with thought
Moulds him an idol of the glittering ore
Or shines his smiling goddess, marble-wrought.

"What bliss for her—e'en on this world of woe
Oh! sire who mak'st yon orb-strown arch thy throne,—
That sees thee, in thy nobles work below,
Shine undefaced!—and calls that work her own!

"This I had hoped: but hope too dear, too great—
Go to thy grave! I feel thee blasted, now—
Give me, fate's sovereign, well to bear the fate
Thy pleasure sends—this, my sole prayer, allow."

XLVI.

Still, fixed on heaven, her earnest eye, all dew,
Seemed as it sought amid the lamps of night
For him her soul addressed; but other view
Far different—sudden from that pensive plight

Recalled her: quick as on primeval gloom
Burst the new day-star, when the Eternal bid,
Appeared, and glowing filled the dusky room,
As 'twere a brillant cloud; the form it hid

Modest emerged, as might a youth beseem;
Save a slight scarf, his beauty bare, and white
As cygnet's bosom on some silver stream;
Or young narcissus, when to woo the light

Of its *first* morn, that flowret open springs;—
And near the maid he comes with timid gaze
And gently fans her, with his full spread wings
Transparent as the cooling gush that plays

From ivory fount. Each bright prismatic tint
Still vanishing, returning, blending, changing,
Glowed, from their fibrous mystic texture glint,
Like colours o'er the full-blown bubble ranging

That pretty urchins launch upon the air
And laugh to see it vanish; yet, so bright,
More like—and even that were faint compare,
As shaped from some new rain-bow; rosy light

Like that which pagans say the dewy car
Precedes of their Aurora, clipp'd him round
Retiring as he mov'd; and evening's star
Shamed not the diamond coronal that bound

His curly locks. And still to teach his face
Expression dear to her he wooed he sought;
And, in his hand, he held a little vase
Of virgin gold in strange devices wrought.

XLVII.

Love toned he spoke, "Fair sister, [FN#17] art thou here
With pensive looks, so near thy bridal bed,
Fixed on the pale cold moon? Nay! do not fear—
To do thee weal o'er mount and stream I've sped.

[FN#17] Sister, was an affectionate appellation, used by the Jews towards all
women.

XLVIII.

"Say, doth thy soul in all its sweet excess
Rush to this bridegroom, smooth and falsehood-taught.
Ah, now! thou yield'st thee to a loathed caress—
While thy heart tells thee loud it owns him not.

XLIX.

"Hadst thou but seen, on Tigris' banks, this morn
Wasting her wild complaints, a wretched maid,
Stung with her wrongs—lone—beauty-reft—forlorn—
And learned 'twas ev'n thy Meles who betrayed,

"Well hadst thou then shrunk to return his love
But wherefore now, on theme of sorrow bide?—
What would thy beauty? here I wait—nay, prove
A spirit's power, nor be my boon denied!

"I'll tell thee secrets of the neither earth
And highest heaven—or dost some service crave?
Declare thy bidding, best of mortal birth,
I'll be thy winged messenger, thy slave." (7)

L.

Then softly Egla, "Lovely being tell—
In pity to the grief thy lips betray
The knowledge of—say with some kindly spell
Dost come from heaven, to charm my pains away?

"Alas! what know'st thou of my plighted lord?
If guilt pollute him, as unless mine ear
Deceive me in the purport of thy word,
Thou mean'st t' imply—kind spirit rest not here

"But to my father hasten and make known
The fearful truth: my doom is his command;
Writ in heaven's book, I guard the oath I've sworn
Unless he will to blot it by thine hand."

LI.

"Thy plight to Meles little need avail."
Zophiel replies: "ere morn, if't be thy will
To Lybian deserts he shall howl his tale
I'll hurl him, at thy word, o'er forest, sea and hill.

LII.

"By all the frauds, which forged in his black breast,
Come forth so white and silvery from his tongue,
My potency he soon shall prove; nor rest
To banquet on the blood of hearts by him unstrung,

"And reft of all their music. Every pain
By him inflicted for his own vile joys
Rend his vile self! fruition not again
Shall crown such arts as now the slave employs!

"But sooth thee, maiden, be thy soul at peace;
Mine be the care to hasten to thy sire
And null thy vow: let every terror cease:
Perfect success attends thy least desire."

LIII.

Then lowly bending with seraphic grace
The vase he proffered full; and not a gem
Drawn forth successive from its sparkling place
But put to shame the Persian diadem.

LIV.

While he "Nay, let me o'er thy white arms bind
These orient pearls less smooth; Egla, for thee,
My thrilling substance pained by storm and wind,
I sought them mid the caverns of the sea.

"And here's a ruby drinking solar rays
I saw it redden on a mountain tip,
Now on thy snowy bosom let it blaze:

31

'Twill blush still deeper to behold thy lip.

"Look, for thy hair a garland; every flower
That spreads its blossoms, watered by the tear
Of the sad slave in Babylonian bower,
Might see its fraid bright hues perpetuate here.

"For morn's light bell, this changeful amythist
A sapphire for the violet's tender blue;
Large opals for the queen-rose zephyr-kist;
And here are emeralds of ev'ry hue
For ev'ry folded bud and leaflet dropped with dew.

LV.

"And here's a diamond cull'd from Indian mine
To gift a haughty queen: it might not be—
I knew a worthier brow, sister divine,
And brought the gem; for well I deem for thee

"The 'arch-chymic sun' in earth's dark bosom wrought
To prison thus a ray; that when dull night
Lours o'er his realms and nature's all seems nought
She whom he grieves to leave may still behold his light." [FN#18]

Thus spake he on, for still the wondering maid
Gazed, as a youthful artist,—rapturously,
Each perfect, smooth, harmonious limb survey'd
Insatiate still her beauty-loving eye.

[FN#18] It was not unusual among the nations of the east, to imitate flowers
with precious stones. The Persian kings about the time of Artaxerxes, sat,
when they gave audience under a vine, the leaves of which were formed of
gold and the grapes of emeralds.

LVI.

For Zophiel wore a mortal form; and blent
In mortal form, when perfect, nature shows
Her all that's fair, enhanc'd; fire, firmament,
Ocean, earth flowers and gems, all there disclose

Their charms epitomized: the heavenly power

To lavish beauty, in this last work crown'd—
And Egla form'd of fibres such as dower
Those who most feel, forgot all else around.

LVII.

He saw, and softening every wily word
Spoke in more melting music to her soul,
And o'er her sense as when the fond night bird
Woos the full rose o'erpowering fragrance stole. (6)

Or when the lillies, sleepier perfume, move,
Disturbed by too young sister-fawns, that play
Among their graceful stalks at morn, and love
From their white cells to lip the dews away.

LVIII.

She strove to speak, but 'twas in murmurs low,
While o'er her cheek, his potent spell confessing,
Deeper diffused the warm carnation glow
Still dewy wet with tears her inmost soul confessing.

As the little reptile, in some lonely grove,
With fixed bright eye of facinating flame
Lures on by slow degrees the plaining dove,
So nearer—nearer still—the bride and spirit came.

LIX.

"Thou, strong, invisible, invidious sprite,
Now, from my love my peerless mortal shield—
What exultation for thy power to night!
Look on thy beauteous charge!—why does she yield?"

LX.

Thus secret he, the pearly bracelet holding,
Lending his lip to accents sweetlier bland

The light that clipt him, half the maid enfolding
Half given—tho' dubious half—her lilly hand.

LXI.

Success seemed his;—but secret, in the height
And pride of transport; as he set at nought
And taunts her guardian power; infernal light
Shot from his eye, with guilt and treachery fraught.

Haply it was but Nature:—she bestows
Intuitive preception, and while art
O'ertasks himself with guile, loves to disclose
The dark soul in the eye, to warn th' o'ertrusting heart.

LXII.

Zophiel, howe'er the warning came, was foiled
What torments burned in his unearthly breast!
The while her trembling hand—untouched, recoiled,
That, wild, exulting glance, the wily fiend confest.

LXIII.

Faintly he spoke—"'Tis Meles' step I here,
Guilty thou know'st him—wilt receive him still?"—
The rosy blood driven to her heart by fear
She said, in accents faint, but firm, "I will."

LXIV.

The spirit heard; and all again was dark;
Save, as before, the melancholy flame
Of the full moon; and faint, unfrequent spark
Which from the perfume's burning embers came.

That stood in vases round the room disposed;
Shuddering and trembling to her couch she crept,—
Soft oped the door and quick again was closed,
And thro' the pale grey moon-light Meles stept.

LXV.

But ere he yet, in haste, could throw aside
His broidered belt and sandals—dread to [illegible]
Eager he sprang—he sought to clasp his bride—
He stopt—a groan was heard—he gasped and fell

LXVI.

Low by the couch of her who widowed lay
Her ivory hands convulsive clasped in prayer,
But lacking power to move; and when 'twas day,
A cold black corse was all of Meles, there.

END OF THE FIRST CANTO.

NOTES.

(1) Wandered malignant o'er the erring earth.

This passage and, indeed the whole poem, is founded on a belief, prevalent in the earlier ages of christianity, that all nations, except the descendents of Abraham, were abandoned by the Almighty, and subjected to the power of daemons or evil spirits. Fontenelle in his *"Histoire des Oracles"* makes the following extract from the works of the Pagan philosopher Porphyry.

"Auguste deja vieux and songeant a se choisir un successeur, alla consulter l'oracle de Delphes. L'oracle ne repondoit point, quiqu 'Auguste n'epargnat pas de sacrifices. A la fin, cependant, il en tira cette reponse. L'enfant Hebreu a qui tous les Dieux obeissent, me chasse d'ici, and me ronvoie dans les Enfers. Sors de ce temple sans parler."

(2) While friendly shades the sacred rites enshroud.

The captive Jews, though they sometimes outwardly conformed to the religion of their oppressors, were accustomed to practice their own in secret.

(3) When fiercer spirits howled, he but complained.

So Milton. Others more mild retreated to a silent valley singing,
With notes angelical, to many a harp,
Their own heroic deeds and hapless fall.

(4) Weary he fainted thro' the toilsome hours,
And then his mystic nature he sustained
On steam of sacrifices, breath of flowers.

Eusebe dans sa "Preparation Evangelique" raporte quantite de passages de Porphyre, ou ce philosophe Payen assure que les mauvais demons sont les auteurs des enchantemens, des philtres, et des malefices; que le mensonge est essentiel a leur nature; qu'ils ne font que tromper nos yeux par des spectres et par des fautomes; qu'ils excitent en nous la plupart de nos passions; qu'ils ont l'ambition de vouloir passer pour des dieux; que leurs corps *aeriens se nourissent* de *fumigations de sand repandu et de la graisse des sacrifices;* qu'il n'y a qu'eux qui se melent de rendre des oracles, et a qui cette fonction pleine de tromperic soit tombee en partage.

Fontenelle, Historie des Oracles.

Still true
To one dear theme, my full soul flowing o'er
Would find no room for thought of what it knew
(5) Nor picturing forfeit transport curse me more.

Si l'homme (says a modern writer) constant dans ses affections, pouvoit saus cesse fournir a un sentiment renouvele sans cesse, sans doute la solitude and l'amour l'egaleroient a Dieu meme; car ce sont la les deux eternel plaisirs du gran Etre.

A celebrated female, (Saint Theresa) used to describe Satan as an unhappy being, who never could know what it was to love.

*(6)And o'er her sense as when the fond night bird
   Woos the full rose o'erpowering fragrance stole.*

This allusion must be familiar to every general reader of poetry.

"The nightingale if he sees the rose becomes intoxicated; he lets go from his hand the reins prudence."
   Fable of the Gardener and Nightingale.

Lady Montague also translates a song, if my memory does not deceive me, thus,

"The nightingale now hovers amid the flowers, her passion is to seek roses."

And from the poet Hafiz,

"When the roses wither and the bower loses its sweetness, you have no longer the tale of the nightingale."

Indeed the rose, in Oriental poetry, is seldom mentioned without her paramour the nightingale, which gives reason to suppose that this bird, in those countries where it was first celebrated, had really some natural fondness for the rose; or perhaps for some insect which took shelter in it. In Sir W. Jones' translation of the Persian fable, of "The Gardener and Nightingale" we meet with the following distich.

_"I know not what the rose says under his lips, that he brings back the helpless Nightingales with their mournful notes.

One day the Gardener, according to his established custom, went to view the roses; he saw a plaintive nightingale rubbing his head on the leaves of the roses and tearing asunder, with his sharp bill, that volume adorned with gold."_

And Gelaleddin Ruzbehar,

"While the nightingale sings thy praises with a loud voice, I am all ear like the stalk of the rosetree."

Pliny, however, in his delightful description of this bird, says nothing, I believe, about the rose.

(7) Les Perses semblent etre les premiers hommes connus de nous qui parlerent des anges comme d'huissiers celestes, et de porteurs d'ordres.

Voltaire, Essai sur les moeurs et l'esprit des nations.

In composing this ode, which was done four years ago, the writer had not the most remote idea, of complimenting any one. Without the slightest pretensions to "connoiseurship" she has only described the absolute effect of the pictures alluded to, on an individual, and would only be considered in the light of an insent warming itself in the sun, and grateful for his pervasive influence.

ODE.

Thou who wert born of Psyche and of Love
And fondly nurst on Poesy's warm breast
    Painting, oh, power adored!
    My country's sons have poured
To thee their orisons; and thou hast blest
Their votive sighs, nor vainly have they strove.

Thou who art wont to soothe the varied pain
That ceaseless throbs at absent lover's heart,
    Who first bestowed thine aid
    On the young Rhodian maid [FN#19]
When doomed, from him whose love was life, to part,
From a lone bard accept an humble heartfelt strain.

[FN#19] I do not positively recollect whether the incident, here described is supposed to have transpired at Rhodes, Corinth, or some other place, and have not, at present, the means for ascertaining. Painting is called the Rhodian Art, but I know not if on account of its having been first invented there or for the eminence of the painters which Rhodes produced; which was so great that an illustrious enemy refrained from burning the city, which he had in his power, out of respect to the genius of Protogenes one of its most celebrated artists.

'Twas the last night the idol youth might stay—
E'en now, to bear him from the rosy isle, [FN#20]

38

The galley waits: he sleeps
She silent wakes and weeps—
Watches his lips that in light dreaming smile—
Twines her soul round his charms and dreads the coming day.

The dazzling drops her pitious eyes that blind
Hushing her struggling sobs she wiped away:—
Her tapers paly light
Fell on the marble white,
Beside the couch where half reclined he lay
And of his beauteous face the shadow well defined.

Loved deity, then first thou cam'st on earth!—
Pity for truth in sorrow, called thee here!
Sudden the fair, inspired,
With a new thought was fired
Her hand urged on by hope—yet, breathing not for fear—
She traced the unreal shade—'twas hers—an art had birth.

[FN#20] Rhodes, in the Greek tongue, signifies *rose* or roses. After being
made the scene of the loves of Venus and Apollo, the isle (says Demoustier)
became an enchanting garden, and soon took the name of the flowers it
produced.

By dearest, tenderest feelings still allured,
Thou sought'st our wilds far blooming o'er the deep
Pleased with the soft employ
A fair haired cherub boy
O'er a more helpless child his watch to keep
Was placed; and from his sports the long restraint endured.

Fair as the hues of heaven, the innocent
Lay like a phantom born of some mild soul;
A drop, for it had wept
A moment ere it slept,
O'er its light vermil cheek was seen to roll
And its young guardian's heart drank beauty as he leant.

That nameless wish to nought but genius known.—
Indefinite—but in each fibre felt,
Whispered. The boy elate
Burned to perpetuate
The full pervasive bliss; enrapt he knelt—
Thou saw'st—a pencil's by—and infant West's thine own.

Soon the plumed savage, from his leafy home

Emerging, saw and loved the gifted child,
    And soon, beneath their care,
    His hands the tints prepare,
That strain their shapely limbs, in grandeur wild
As thro' their arching woods, the desert warriors roam.[FN#21]

[FN#21] Sir Benjamin West, when a child, was presented with the primitive colours by an Indian. See Galt's Life of West.

Please he repaid their plans, nor those alone;
Sped by his strength the painted arrow flew;
    And oft the soaring bird
    For shape, or hue preferred,
To make a model for his art he knew
While sovereign Nature saw—and smiled upon her throne.

Bold Science, who earth's caverned depths explores,
And soars triumphant 'mid new worlds of light,—
    Lays bare the heaving heart [FN#22]
    Nor suffers life to part—
Lures the red lightning from its stormy height—
Oft, goddess kneels to thee to save his precious stores.

[FN#22] An operation was performed at Paris by M. Richerande in which the heart of a patient, who afterwards recovered, was laid bare.

The rough-browed warrior on the midnight deck
While stealing softness thro' his pulses glides,
    By the moon's pensive rays
    Regards with lengthened gaze,
The pictured form his scarry bosom hides
By day; that tho' death grasp, hangs smiling at his neck.

When fate has torn from the fond mother's arms
The tender hope her bosom fed, to thee
    She flies;—and ere decay
    Can mar his beauteous prey
Her arching eyes, amid their grief, can see,
Still dawning bright, to them, its early-blighted charms.

The generous youth who, fired by love of fame,
A victim at her bloody altars fell;
    To the beloved ones reft,
    By aid of thee, has left
His form, his lip, his ardent glance, to tell
How fair was he on earth who left it for a name.

The patriot—here a moment let my strain
Tremble before thy Stuart—who but he
    Could bid mild Washington—
    His god-loved labours done—
Thus sit before us breathing majesty,
And, in his deep blue eye, still life and soul retain?

Methinks, the while I gaze, each graceful line
So light imprinted on his forehead fair,
    Where Wisdom sits serene
    Of every sense the queen,
Seems as an embryo empire still were there,
While still his ample breast swells with the vast design.

And fondly o'er the mellow tints I pause
Of her, whose vivid touch shames not her sire;
    Bold Genius in his pride
    Has marked her as his bride,
On his bright pinions bids her soul aspire,
Nor pay the tribute due by tardier Nature's laws. [FN#23]

[FN#23] While composing this ode the writer was shown a beautiful
specimen from the hand of a young daughter of the celebrated Stuart, who
entirely devoted herself to the art.

But guard thee well young J—e: in his embrace
How many seal with death their ectasy!
    Too deep, intense, and wild,
    For one so late a child,
I fear me lest the proffered transport be
That every earthlier joy absorbent would efface.

Soft is thy form—amid the unpent air,
Pay rosy exercise her just demands:
    Tho' heaven thy lone hours woo
    Earth still demands her due;
Gay health to guard e'en genius' palace stands—
And when she takes her flight—e'en genius, must despair.

Nor those alone doomed to incarnate birth
Painting, death-baffler, is it thine to save!
    The heavenly shapes that flit,
    When the entranced fit,
Is on, and the charmed soul forgets its earth,
Thou bidst to earthly eyes their sky-dipt vestments wave.

The radiant visions Fancy's wand uprears
When Poesy around has spread her spell,
    Like summer flowrets dies
    Refresh the enchanted skies,
Where, soft as air, and lovelier for her fears,
Bright in her golden robes flies fair-haired Florimell. [FN#24]

[FN#24] The flight of Florimell, from a scene in Spencer's Faery Queen, is an exquisite little picture by Allston, in the possession of a private gentleman.

The miracles, in holy record kept, Done—
ere one cheering ray of distant light
    Thro' death's dark portals shown,
    At thy command alone,
Still, still—reacted meet—the astonished sight,
Tho' rolling ages o'er the scene have swept.

In this far distant land, which the great deep
Perchance embosomed, when that dust was rife,
    The pale unconscious dead
    On the strown relics laid
Of old Elisha, in his passing sleep,
Still, at the hallowed touch, starts back to warmth and life. [FN#25]

[FN#25] Every one must recollect the sublime picture here alluded to.

Sweet, when the soul is weary of the ills
That stern reality presents, to dwell
    On beauteous forms: they smooth
    The ruffled sense, and sooth
The heart with soft perfection; till a spell
Blends with its troublous pulse, and all its achings stills.

And who can look nor own the pencil's power
Where tender Ariadne, happy yet, [FN#26]
    Lies in a dream of bliss?
    The last half-pitying kiss,
By falsehood given, her sleeping lip has met—
That still seems hovering there like Zephyr o'er a flower.

[FN#26] Vanderlyn's Ariadne.

The dawn breaks slowly o'er the distant main,
To come no more her ingrate hero flies;
    While thoughts confiding speak
    Upon her mantling cheek—

Illusion chains the sense—in lowest sighs
Whispering—we fear to see her wake to pain.

But whither wandering? whatsoe'er has gained
Long conning book and heart the white-haired sage;
      Cause and remote effect
      In living semblance dect,
The truths divine of many a moral page
Thy hand, harmonious Peale, hath at a glance explained.

STANZAS.

To meet a friendship such as mine
Such feelings must thy heart refine
As seldom mortal mind gives birth,
'Tis love, without a stain of earth,
      Fratello del mio cor.

Tho' friendship be its earthly name
All pure, from highest heaven, it came
'Tis never felt for more than one,
And scorns to dwell with Venus' son
      Fratello del mio cor.

Him let it view not, or it flies
Like tender hues of morning-skies,
Or morn's sweet flower, of purple glow.
When sunny beams too ardent grow
      Fratello del mio cor.

It's food is looks, its nectar, sighs,
Its couch the lip, its throne the eyes
The soul its breath; and so possest,
Heaven's raptures reign in mortal breast.
      Fratello del mio cor.

ON THE DEATH OF A LADY.

Thy home seemed not of earth—so blest—
  But there has fall'n a shaft of fate—
The dove is stricken; and the nest
  She warmed and cheered is desolate.

But fairest not for thee, we mourn:
  Blest from thy birth, thou still art so—
The tear must dew thine early urn
  For him whom thou hast taught to know

The zest of joys—complete, as knows
  Thy vital flame, the pang that tost
And changed thee past, where now it glows—
  Knowing, yet feeling all is lost.

There is a flower of tender white
  And, on its spotless bosom, play
The moon's soft beams, one lovely night;
  But when appears the morning ray

'Tis shut and withered—even now
Around your lime I see it wave; [FN#27]
'Tis pure, and fresh, and fair, as thou—
And sinks in beauty to its grave.

[FN#27] The white convolvulus; it blossoms just after sun-set, and is seen in great abundance entwining the lime-hedges, about the plantations of Cuba.